THE FOUR
DONKEYS

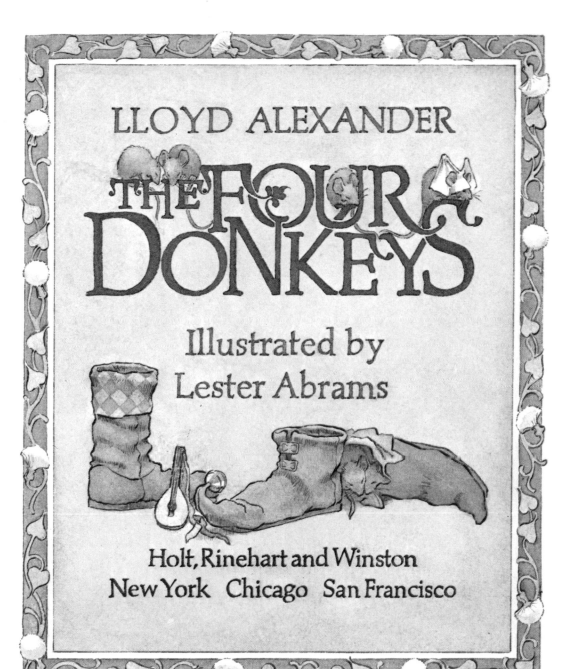

LLOYD ALEXANDER

THE FOUR DONKEYS

Illustrated by
Lester Abrams

Holt, Rinehart and Winston
New York Chicago San Francisco

The Prydain Chronicles by Lloyd Alexander
The Book of Three
The Black Cauldron
The Castle of Llyr
Taran Wanderer
The High King

The Prydain Picture Books
Coll and His White Pig
The Truthful Harp

Other Books by Lloyd Alexander
The Four Donkeys
Time Cat

A Holt Reinforced Edition
Copyright © 1972 by Lloyd Alexander
Copyright © 1972 by Lester Abrams
All rights reserved, including the right to reproduce
this book or portions thereof in any form.
Published simultaneously in Canada by Holt, Rinehart
and Winston of Canada, Limited.
ISBN: 0-03-089516-2
Library of Congress Catalog Card Number: 70-150029
Printed in the United States of America
Designed by Susan Mann
Published, November, 1972
Second Printing, March, 1975

With gratitude for all wise donkeys
Lloyd Alexander

To Susan
Lester Abrams

ONE MORNING,
a Tailor, a Baker, and a Shoemaker, each on his own, set out for the town fair.

JUST AS THE TAILOR was ready to leave, the Baker came bursting into the shop, bellowing to have his jacket mended.

"I've no time today," the Tailor protested. "I can't be late for the fair."

"Nor can I!" cried the Baker, pounding on the counter and making such a racket that the Tailor could only do as he asked.

Thinking the Baker's manners were even lumpier than his cheesecakes, the Tailor stitched away as fast as he could. "Oh, that horrible jacket! Oh dear, oh dear," he muttered to his pet otter. "I hate the very sight of it! True, I made the thing for him in the first place. But only because he'd have it no other way. The fellow's baking is bad enough, but his taste in clothing is worse!"

At last rid of the Baker and his hideous jacket, the Tailor packed up his bolts of cloth, shears, and iron. Shouldering the bundle, he hurried out of the shop and started off on the road to the fair.

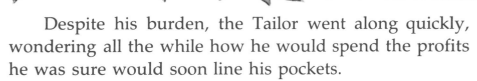

Despite his burden, the Tailor went along quickly, wondering all the while how he would spend the profits he was sure would soon line his pockets.

"A new ironing board? A new cutting table? A new kitchen stove for my wife?"

The Tailor snapped his fingers. "No! Best yet, a way to have all and more. A signboard to hang outside my shop!

"Just so," he chattered on. "The biggest, brightest signboard, and my name in the boldest lettering. That's bound to draw more customers. I'll have all the fashionable folk at my door, even the Mayor himself!"

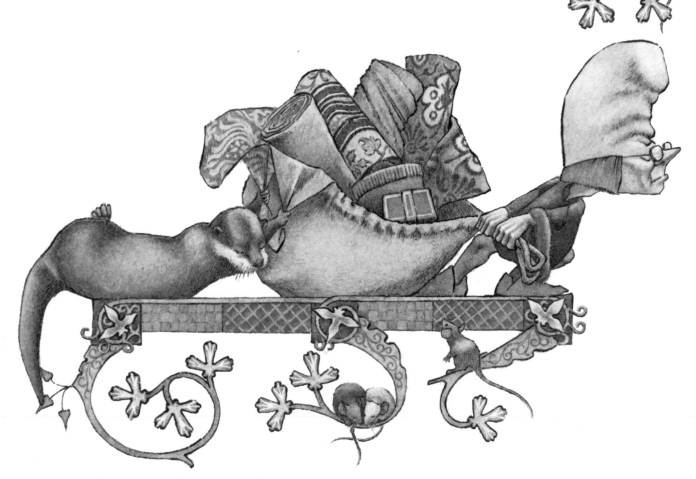

The Tailor stepped briskly, humming his favorite little tune. However, before he had gone halfway, his feet began smarting and stabbing as if both shoes were full of needles. And he could do nothing but sit down at the side of the road and nurse his tender toes.

"I can thank the Shoemaker for my pains," he moaned. "He made these shoes too narrow! Oh, he's a fine cobbler, if you like bunions and blisters!"

THE MORNING OF THE FAIR, the Shoemaker had risen early and was already well on his way before daybreak. Rolls of leather, hammer and nails, tacks and pegs, all neatly strapped to his back. The door padlocked behind him. Nothing overlooked. "First at the fair, first to strike the bargain." He chuckled to himself. No doubt of it, he was the shrewdest fellow in the world.

"And the best in my trade," he added. "That last pair of shoes for the Tailor? A masterpiece!"

As for the profits he knew he would make, the
Shoemaker had already decided how to spend them.

"A gold ring! There's nothing like a fine piece of
jewelry to show a man's success. Wait till the neighbors
see it shining on my finger! Especially that witless Baker
who thinks himself such a peacock in his fancy clothes!"

On he went, whistling through his teeth. But the
Shoemaker had been up so early that after a while his
eyes felt heavy. He began yawning and blinking. At last,
he stopped and sat down against a milestone.

"I'm in plenty of time," he said. "No harm in forty
winks to sharpen my wits."

He shut his eyes and soon was fast asleep, dream-
ing of the ring he would buy.

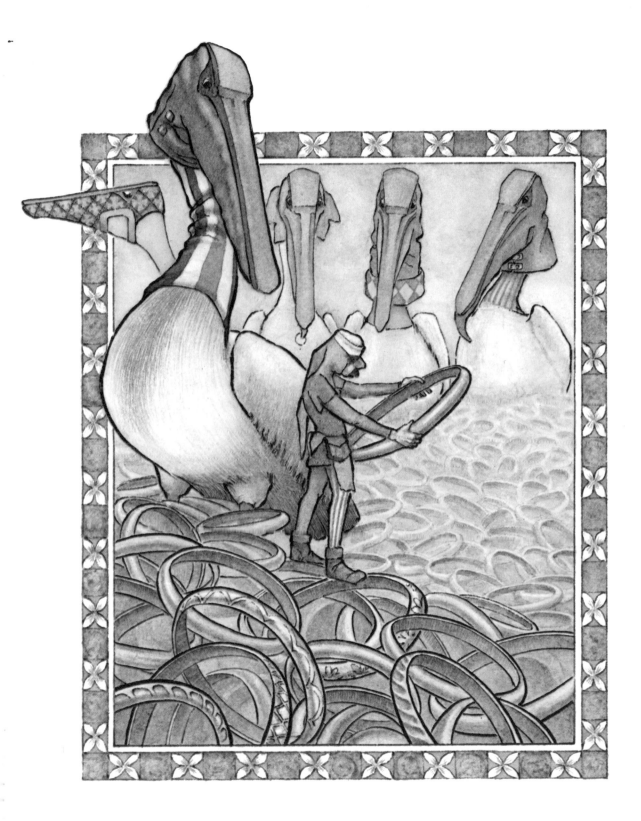

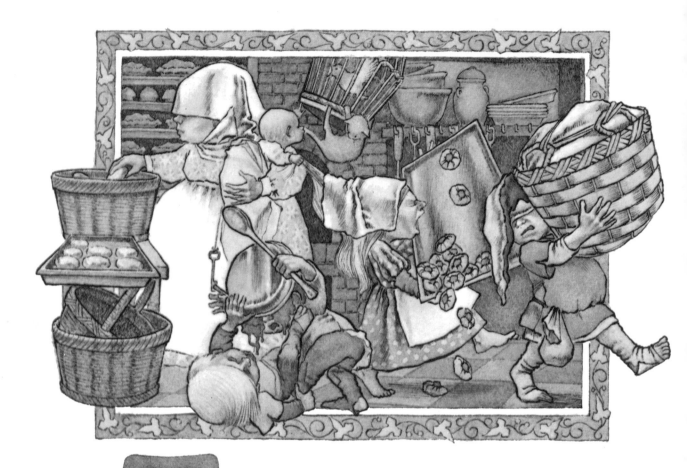

THAT SAME MORNING, when the Baker at last climbed into his cart and headed for the fair, he felt light as a lemon pie and cheerful as a cherry tart. He gave his donkey a merry slap with the reins and began singing at the top of his voice. After a late start, he was more than making up for lost time. What a morning it had been! First, the seam of his best jacket had split. Then,

his three boys had begun punching each other's noses; and his three girls pulling each other's hair. To top it off, his wife declared she had mending enough. So he could only run to the Tailor's shop. What a fuss the under-done little fellow had made over half a dozen stitches!

That finished, the Baker decided it would be wise to pack more baskets of bread, a double supply of tarts, and some trays of frosted cookies for good measure.

"They'll go faster than hot cakes," the Baker said to himself. "Nobody has my touch with a rye loaf or a raisin bun; and my pies are worth their weight in gold. They'll surely make a fortune for me today."

Loading his cart, however, had stirred his appetite for a second breakfast that took longer than his first. Even now, amid such delicious aromas, the Baker could not keep himself from stuffing cookies into his mouth.

At last on his way, he jogged along in his cart, munching and singing at the same time. Crossing the bridge, he winked at his reflection in the stream below.

"Now there," he said, "I won't deny it. That's the handsomest jacket ever I've seen on a fine figure of a man. But, to put the sweetest frosting on the cake, I must have a new hat to go with it. And I'll order a new pair of boots from the Shoemaker. Before the day's out, I'll sell enough raspberry tarts alone to buy whatever finery I want."

He began to sing again, but stopped in surprise a moment later. Just ahead, he saw the Tailor sitting by the road. As the Baker drew closer, the Tailor limped toward the cart and waved his arms.

"Stop! Oh, stop!" cried the Tailor. "It's my feet!"

"Of course they're your feet," replied the Baker, pulling up, and not at all happy at being delayed. "And you have a pair of them, so what are you whining about?"

"They hurt! Oh, you should see the blisters," moaned the Tailor.

"Your blisters are no business of mine," returned the Baker. "If that's all you stopped me for, then good day to you."

"But I can't walk," the Tailor whimpered. "Let me ride in your cart."

"Oho," said the Baker, at last catching the thread of the Tailor's complaints. "If you want to ride with me, you must pay for it. A place in my cart? Sixpence!"

He saw the Tailor's face go sour at having to part with what was only a fair fee. And, thought the Baker, as peevish as he was to me this morning! He's skinny as a breadstick, but he has twice the crust!

Pocketing the coins the Tailor reluctantly handed him, the Baker shouted: "Jump up! Off we go! Mind you don't squash my chocolate eclairs with all that stuff of yours."

As the Tailor squeezed in behind him, the Baker felt more than ever pleased with himself. "I've done well," he thought, "and made a profit even before I'm at the fair. So, why not buy a fancy vest to go with my new boots and my new hat?"

He slapped the reins, the cartwheels creaked under the added burden, and off they went down the road.

When the Shoemaker awoke from his nap, the sun was high. He jumped to his feet, dismayed and alarmed. Time saved? Time lost! Vexed at oversleeping, at being late, and having no one to blame but himself, he could think of no way to reach the fair fast enough.

That instant, he saw the Baker's cart come around the bend. He ran eagerly toward it and called to the Baker to stop.

"What, you too?" said the Baker. "A ride in my cart? Sixpence, then. That's what I charged the Tailor."

Hearing this, the Shoemaker retorted, "Your fee pinches worse than a tight boot. The Tailor paid sixpence? I'll give you a third of that. Even that's generous as I'm not going a quarter of the distance."

Handing him the coins, and leaving the puzzled Baker counting on his fingers, the Shoemaker sprang into the cart. The Tailor, he saw, had selfishly taken up nearly all the room with his pack. Nevertheless, by shoving, pushing, and squeezing as hard as he could, the Shoemaker wedged himself and his pack into the little space that was left, and impatiently called out: "What's this, a snail wagon? I've paid my fare. Now let's get on! I've important business waiting."

The wheels creaked and groaned louder than before. The sides of the cart bulged, the floorboard sagged, and the axles bent almost to the ground The Baker slapped the reins.

The donkey sat down in the middle of the road.

At this, the Tailor, in tears of despair, wrung his hands and pleaded with the animal to get up. The Shoemaker stamped his foot and cursed his luck at falling in with a pair of fools and a stubborn donkey. The Baker shouted and slapped the reins all the harder.

The donkey only settled more heavily on his haunches—out of wind, out of strength, unwilling to budge another inch.

The Tailor clapped his hands to his head. "Oh dear, oh dear, whatever shall I do? My signboard! I'll never get to the fair! Thanks to you, Shoemaker! First, I go lame in your shoes; then, you come crowding in with your great pack of rubbish!"

"If it hadn't been for your great sack of rubbish that weighs more than it's worth," snapped the Shoemaker, "I'd have a gold ring on my finger by now."

"If it hadn't been for the two of you," cried the Baker, "I'd be wearing a new hat and vest!" A moment earlier, the Baker had been congratulating himself on his unforeseen gains. Now it dawned on him that he stood to lose all his profit and ruin his donkey besides. To add a sour icing to the matter, he heard the Shoemaker yammering for his money back.

"Money back?" roared the Baker, shaking a fist. "The little you paid won't make up for my troubles. I would have given you an order for a pair of boots. Now I'll give you something else, you leatherhead!"

"Leatherhead?" cried the Shoemaker. "Lumpkin!"

"Dear sirs! Gentlemen! Neighbors!" piped up the Tailor, afraid the two might come to serious blows and delay them even longer. "This doesn't move the donkey!"

The Baker lowered his fist, realizing the Tailor had put the matter in a nutshell. His next thought was to lighten the load by tossing out their packs along with the Tailor and Shoemaker themselves. Even that would serve no purpose. Any fool could see the donkey was altogether exhausted.

"We'll have to go our own ways," grumbled the Shoemaker. "Every man for himself, and leave the creature where he sits."

"Oh no, you won't!" burst out the Baker. "You're both to blame. Try walking off, either one of you, and I'll thump you like dough!"

The Shoemaker was wise enough to know the stout Baker would keep his word. So he said bitterly: "We can't stay and we can't go. The donkey doesn't move, neither do we. So, there's only one way. Put him in the cart. He won't pull us. We'll have to pull him."

The Tailor wailed that he was a man of delicate health. The Baker kneaded his forehead, befuddled at the notion of trading places with his own donkey. But, since neither had a better plan, they could only agree with the Shoemaker.

Straining and struggling, heaving and hauling, grunting and grumbling, the Tailor, the Baker, and the Shoemaker hoisted the weary donkey, still on his haunches, into the cart. While the donkey brayed astonishment at being so well treated for the first time in his long years, the three set off again, dragging all the load behind them.

For some while, deep in their own miseries, they only glared at each other. Then the Tailor stumbled and would have fallen flat on his face. The Baker grudgingly reached out a burly arm to help him along. The Tailor was too surprised to do more than gasp "Thank you," and he was all the more astonished when the Baker actually grinned at him.

Limping on, however, the Tailor's feet began smarting worse than ever. "Now," he moaned, "there's not enough room in my shoes for my blisters!"

They halted a moment and, without even being asked, the Shoemaker, a little less gruff than he had been, softened the Tailor's shoes with some oil.

"Oh, that's much better," the Tailor sighed gratefully, thinking the Shoemaker was not really such a bad sort after all. "But the poor donkey! If his hoofs hurt as much as my toes, no wonder he couldn't go farther!"

The Baker's jacket had been made for leisure, not labor. Soon, he felt the seams rip one by one until his magnificent garment was as tattered as a scarecrow's. But his spirits rose when the Tailor promised to mend it later, good as new and free of charge. Nevertheless, the Baker's arms and legs ached with his efforts.

"I'd rather knead a thousand loaves!" he cried, puffing and gasping. "If I were my donkey, I'd have given my last heehaw by now!"

The Shoemaker had overlooked only one thing before leaving for the fair: his breakfast. As the day wore on, he began groaning over his empty stomach.

Ashamed to ask for food, he was delighted to find the Baker to be quicker-witted than he had thought. For the Baker, seeing his distress, cheerfully gave him his fill of bread and pastry.

This satisfied the Shoemaker's hunger, but did nothing for his sore shoulders, where the harness chafed and rubbed.

"I'll never curse a donkey," muttered the Shoemaker, "now that I've carried his load!"

At last, they glimpsed rooftops and steeples. Almost at their goal, they forced themselves to go as fast as they could, stumbling and slipping in their haste to reach the fair. Closer and closer they hurried and finally, saving their last breath for three cheers of triumph, they struggled into the town.

Then they stopped and stared.

The market place was empty. The bright banners they had expected to see had all been taken down. The buyers were gone. The fair was over.

The Tailor sniffled. "That new hat and vest would have been most becoming with your jacket," he sighed to the Baker. "And you, Master Shoemaker, alas for your gold ring."

"Alas for your signboard," answered the Shoemaker, ruefully. "But, never fear, your fame will spread without it."

"You can be sure it will," the Baker added, as cheerfully as he could. "But I know how both of you feel, for I feel the same. Still, there's always the next fair."

It was after nightfall when they started back, because the Tailor, worried that the donkey might catch a chill, had insisted on taking time to sew a splendid blanket for him. The Shoemaker, not forgetting his own raw shoulders, had cobbled a comfortable new harness. The Baker had managed to find a feed store open and had traded his cakes for a nose bag of fresh oats.

The donkey, refreshed by his rest, kicked up his heels, brayed in the best of spirits, and pulled the cart as if it were light as a feather. It very nearly was! Weary as they were, the Tailor, the Baker and the Shoemaker had decided to walk home.

They trudged beside the donkey, glad to let him be their guide. For he knew the road better than any of them.

And so the Tailor, the Baker, and the Shoemaker came home together, a little wiser for having made donkeys of themselves.

ABOUT THE AUTHOR

Lloyd Alexander is among the most popular and distinguished writers for children today. Winner of the National Book Award, Mr. Alexander is the author of nearly a dozen books for young people, including the Newbery Medal winner, THE HIGH KING. He lives with his wife in Philadelphia, Pennsylvania.

ABOUT THE ARTIST

Lester Abrams is passionately devoted to the art of picture-book illustration for children. THE FOUR DONKEYS is his first book. Mr. Abrams received his art training at the Rhode Island School of Design and now lives in Wellfleet on Cape Cod.

ABOUT THE BOOK

The full-color art was camera-separated for printing by off-set. The art is pen-and-ink with watercolor. The text is set in Palatino and the display type is handlettered.